THE URBAN EROTICA
FAIRY TALE COLLECTION

Jack's
Beanstalk

THE URBAN EROTICA
FAIRY TALE COLLECTION

Jack's
Beanstalk

HONEY CUMMINGS

4 Horsemen
Publications, Inc.

4 Horsemen
Publications, Inc.

4 Horsemen Publications, Inc.
1497 Main St. Suite 169
Dunedin, FL 34698
4horsemenpublications.com
info@4horsemenpublications.com

Cover & Typesetting by Battle Goddess Productions
Editior Vanessa Valiente

Audio ISBN: 978-1-64450-209-9
Ebook ISBN: 978-1-64450-210-5
Print ISBN: 978-1-64450-211-2

Dedication

To my personal friend Jenn
and her adventures in exotic bromeliads!

XOXO Honey Cummings

1

Jack Spriggins

"What shall we do, what shall we do?"

Kendall Warden adjusted her miniskirt once more before picking up her martini. Michael, an acquaintance from one of her father's firms, was playing bartender tonight. *At least the view is delightful. Even Axel is lurking about,* she laughed to herself before hunting for her best friend Pearl—the mastermind behind this party.

They had met in high school, and in adulthood, had become closer friends. Then, by some twist of fate, they managed to work together as client and contract lawyer. It made for fun nights in Costa Rica and Holland at elite plant shows as she locked down new customers to sell their exotic variants of bromeliads, while they partied and ate meals with the biggest names in the industry, never turning down a chance to have some fun in a darkened corner.

"Dammit," Pearl whined as she looked at a cherry stain on her white blouse. "And I was being so careful too."

Kendall giggled. "Why on earth would anyone in their right mind eat cherries in a white shirt?"

Pearl smirked, grabbing another from the bowl on the kitchen island before shrugging. "We both know I've never been in my right mind."

"Hey, at least you're at home and can change," Kendall offered before taking a sip of her martini. "Not like you have to drive or stumble upstairs."

"Oh, you're right!" Sucking on the cherry for a moment, Pearl said, "I'll change in a minute."

"Don't forget to lock your room or Axel might slip inside."

Pearl watched as Michael served another round of drinks to a few girls. "What can that man *not* do?"

"Hmm?" Kendall followed her stare. "You referring to the elusive Mister Michael?"

"Yeah, I mean, he's a beast as an advisor at the investor's firm, but..." Pearl sighed as if unsure of her own thoughts. "Where did he have the time to learn bartending? Every day I discover some new skillset that he's flawless at every time."

"I think his sister works as a part-time bartender at Red's. As far as I understood, something bad went down in their hometown, and he's been taking care of her ever since she moved in with him. She has a bad hip or something like that from a car accident." Kendall shrugged, adding her assessment. "He seems like a good guy and a smart man. Mmm...

so much, man, you think he's stacked under all those clothes?"

"He's single, Kendall." Pearl laughed, spitting a cherry pit into her napkin.

Scoffing, Kendall took a silencing sip of her martini. *Yeah...but he has the hots for you, Pearl. For some time now, he's had that hungry look in his eyes. Even when I last spoke to him on the matter, he would do things his way and in time. Perhaps tonight might be the night, and he'll finally find a way to get your attention. If only you knew what was coming...I have been sworn to secrecy!*

"He's fair game," offered Pearl, raising a brow.

"He threw this party for you, Pearl," Kendall breathed before draining the last of her martini. "Something tells me he's aiming *elsewhere*."

"No way." Pearl rolled her eyes. "I mean, he's best friends with Axel, my friends-with-benefits."

"Like that would stop a guy. That just tells him you're single too and a horny bitch." Laughing, Kendall scanned the room and she scowled, "Oh no... speaking of horny and bitchy."

"What?" Pearl froze, her hand hovering over the cherry bowl. "I don't like it when you make that face."

"Who invited Professor Gaston?" Kendall whined.

Taking a cherry, Pearl whispered, "I did."

"Why?" exclaimed Kendall, her shoulders shuddering.

Sucking on the cherry in thought, she finally admitted, "He's great eye candy and fun to flirt with, though at times, a little too forward for my taste."

"He's always a little too forward." Kendall gave her a skeptical look.

Kendall looked back but dodged making eye contact with Gaston. *Shit, shit, shit! Someone else, look at someone else!* At that moment, Axel waved at her when she met his gaze, and she laughed, waving back. *Saved by the horny dork in the far corner. Thanks, Axel!*

I can always count on you for an infamous, awkward wave.

"I can't believe you and Axel are each other's booty call." She glared over at Pearl. "Is he really any good? Or just easy access?"

"What? He has toys," Pearl defended. "He's definitely not relationship material, but I don't think he's actively looking so it's convenient. But I do like that collection he has..."

"Buy some for yourself!" fussed Kendall. "You must be the only woman I know who doesn't own a vibrator or a dildo. Considering you seem the type who likes having a man in control of the toy while he fu—"

"Shhh!" Pearl choked on her cherry. "Dammit, I accidentally swallowed."

"Sure, you *accidentally swallowed*." Kendal smirked, making Pearl flush.

They fell silent as a tall, dark man walked past them, folding out of view as he inspected the array of beers and drinks from the fridge before finally selecting a beer. They had been alone up until this moment, but the stranger's side glance he gave them made it clear of his intrigue of the gossiping girls in the kitchen.

Kendall arched an eyebrow, enjoying how his ass looked in his pants, shooting Pearl a look before lipping, *who is that?*

Pearl shrugged. *I blast-texted every number.* She motioned with her hand as if she sprinkled magic dust over the entire room.

You a horny-bitch, lipped Kendall. *All of them are on your phone? Really?*

Pearl shrugged. "So?"

They started sniggering as the stranger returned his attention to them. He was well over six feet tall, broad shouldered with a striking set of hazel eyes. He might as well been a model from a Ralph Lauren commercial. *Well-dressed and that cologne... I wouldn't mind taking him home or sneaking off for some quick fun.*

Kendall straightened herself, correcting her slouch. She flashed a big smile, *thank you, Lord, for my dark complexion, because I tend to blush more than Pearl in these kind of situations!*

"Good evening, ladies." His deep voice sent a shiver through Kendall. His smile wide, and the dip in his eyes as he appraised her sent an excited flash of heat through her. "So, birthday girl, who's your friend?" He offered his hand, and Kendall obliged as he kissed it. "I don't think we've met."

"My name's Kendall," she answered as heat rose to her face. *He's checking off all the boxes of who my dream man would be. If he escorts me to my car later, I'm in so much trouble.* "And you are?"

"JACK." Clearly, Pearl had been searching for his name as it left her lips, louder than intended.

Chuckling, he nodded. "Jack Spriggins. A pleasure to meet you, Kendall. So, do you work at the firm or are you a client of Pearl's?"

"Childhood friends," she offered.

"Well, I better go change out of this stained shirt," Pearl's voice trailed off as she disappeared through her bedroom door.

Kendall's eye widened, her cheeks puffing out as she glared at the door. *Pearl! Girl, you did me dirty! You almost didn't remember this man's name and now, you're hiding in your bedroom! Punk ass bitch... I see you.*

"Oh, I guess it's just the two of us. So, childhood friends, that's pretty awesome." He took a sip of his beer, his hazel eyes searching her face. "I don't think I've seen you around the firm before."

"Y-yeah." Kendall's nerves tightened. *Damn you, Pearl! I needed a wingman for just a bit longer!* "And I suppose you can also say we collaborate on important business trips. Um, so Jack, what do you do for a living? You work at the firm, then?"

He cringed. "Well, I did, until...I was part of that wave of layoffs last month."

"That sucks." Kendall tilted her head, curious at his transparent reply. "Sorry to hear that. How's the job hunt going?"

"Yeah, not so great. I haven't found anything promising, and it's looking like I might have to roll-up my sleeves and get my hands dirty." He shrugged, guzzling his beer a little harder as his charisma faltered.

"Dirty? How so?" He now had Kendall's attention. *What I wouldn't give for you to get dirty with me by the end of the night...*

"I don't like going too long without a steady income, so I usually grab a labor job in between the corporate ones." He thumbed the label on the beer bottle, their roles flipping as he became the nervous one. "Anyhow, Kendall, it was nice meeting you. Hopefully, we cross paths later." Without warning, he spun away, his face hidden from her as he added, "Bye."

"Wait—" With that, he was gone without another word. *Really? Self-rejecting before I had a say in the matter? Granted, I had planned to reject you when you mentioned you were laid off? Because, a jobless man comes with risks. But still... someone with a plan is another matter. Wonder what Michael thinks of—*

"Well, if it isn't Kendall!" Gaston's voice sent a harrowing shiver up her spine. "I haven't seen you since my Business Proposals course."

Inhaling deep, Kendall faced him and said flatly, "Professor Gaston. Imagine meeting you here. How's your girlfriend doing?" *Please tell me you have one so I can lower my guard. Weren't you chasing the English Literature Professor across the hall from you? Pray-tell she folded to your advances.*

"No woman can tie this bull down," he announced.

FUCK. He's been rejected, I see. Can't say I blame her for saying hell no *to him.* Wincing, Kendall searched the room. *Michael's making drinks and has his back turned, Axel has a hand up some girl's skirt, Pearl must be taking a damn shower at this rate, the catering dude has already left to take a call on his cell, and...*

"There you are!" Jack's booming voice caught her by surprise, the heat of his hand soft against the small of her back. "I lost you for a moment there, baby. Didn't realize you were in a conversation with... mister? I'm sorry, have we met?"

Baby? Kendall looked up at her towering savior in awe. *Wait, had he noticed my panic, then circled back to save me? What a gentleman! Regained some points there, Mr. Tall-Dark-And-Handsome.*

"Professor Gaston, and you are?" Kendall tensed at the aggression in Gaston's voice, and Jack pulled her into him.

His two massive hands squeezed firm. The crushing exchange made the threads of his muscles flex in both forearms. Jack flashed a grin, and Gaston cleared his voice as if signaling their shift into the second round.

Kendall snorted before rolling her eyes. *Sometimes, I feel like I should take bets when shit like this goes down.*

"Jack Spriggins, Kendall's boyfriend," he announced with utter confidence.

Kendall's smile strained. She turned her head slow, eyebrows rising high. *What? Did he just... he just called himself...* Blinking, she puffed out her cheeks, her brow furrowing in disbelief. *My boyfriend?*

"Oh?" Gaston released the shake, then took a step back as if there were guidelines on how close he should be to a claimed woman. "Nice to meet you. I thought you came alone…"

Creeper! Did he watch me from the parking lot or something? "He had to work late…" Kendall shrugged and rubbed Jack's back. *Oh my, the muscles on this man's back! Does he workout with Axel and Michael? Either way, at least he was able to force Gaston to back off. I should remember to bring up my "boyfriend" if Gaston tries this again. Even if I still don't have one.*

"I rode in with Axel," Jack offered, his hand sliding to her hip. "But I suppose I'll have to play designated driver tonight if you continue to drink those martinis now, huh, honey?"

"Oh?" Kendall let her hand slip down his back until she could squeeze an ass cheek, making him choke on his beer. "How many martinis do you think I've had? I'm not here to get shitfaced, baby."

"I was hoping to have a little fun later." Jack winked, his eyes searching her face as he returned the gesture and goosed her.

Kendall yelped and covered her mouth. *He did not just pinch my ass!*

Gaston scoffed. "Well, you two lovebirds enjoy your evening. I see someone I need to say hello to."

He's leaving! YES! It worked!

2

Climbing the Beanstalk

"Two in each hand and one in my mouth"

K endall turned her attention back to Jack. *Well, I didn't take him for a smooth operator after his earlier defeat,* she marveled at his intuition.

Her hand glided back toward his back, his muscles hard underneath his shirt. Face hot with lustful thoughts, she admired the moment of authority he had taken with Gaston. Kendall's body buzzed with desire. *Maybe he'd be in the mood for a quick hookup at the very least... dammit, Pearl! You've corrupted me with all your 'let's have a little fun' on a whim.* Inhaling deep, Gaston was finally out of view, and she hadn't seen exactly where Jack had appeared from. *Regardless, I think he secured me immunity from Gaston for the night, if not for a while!*

Kendall hugged Jack, relief washing over her. "Thank you! You saved me!"

"Sorry, if I only knew leaving you alone would bring over the only shark in the room," he glanced over to the hall where Gaston had disappeared down and snorted. "I would've braved talking with you longer."

"No, no. I just...didn't want to entertain his forwardness tonight." She broke away, frowning at her empty martini glass. *Come on, Kendall. You can't start with, 'So you wanna? Wink, wink.'*

"Speaking of forwardness." He lifted an eyebrow, giving her a smug expression. "I wasn't expecting you to rub up on me like that, then squeeze my ass."

Biting her lip, it was her turn to dip her eyes up and down to devour the view. "Well, I can't say I didn't find you attractive too, Mr. Spriggins."

"Is that so, Ms. Kendall," he mimicked. "Do you need an escort to your car? He might try to follow you there too."

Kendall placed the glass down. *I've only had three drinks tonight, but it might just be enough liquid courage. Before I leave, I want a taste of what this man has to offer. Show me your world, Jack. Are you willing to trade a cow for some magic beans tonight? This hot mama's hoping that by the time we make it to the...* "Yes. Walk me to my car." She grabbed the beer from his hand, setting it on the counter, then pulled him behind her.

"Hey, I at least wanted to finish that." He let her tug him down the hall, passing the leering Gaston and out the door. "Are you that worked up over the professor?"

"You can say that" Kendall snorted. "But it's not Gaston that has me flustered." She winked up at Jack as she pressed the elevator button.

"Is that so?" Jack's grin widened, briefly looking away before meeting her gaze again. "Are you leading me into a dark corner somewhere to play?"

Kendall shrugged, feigning shy. "Maybe..."

The elevator opened. No one but them slipped inside as the doors closed. As it began descending ten floors toward level 2 parking, she wasted no time. *I want him now, not later.* Fisting his shirt, she tugged his lips to hers, bending Jack to her will. He followed her lead, opening the gates just as her tongue entered the hot crevasse. She moaned as his heated hands glided to her ass cheeks, squeezing tight, pressing her into his body.

He backed her into the corner of the elevator. The numbers counting down behind them as she sucked on his tongue. Her breasts pressed against the hard planes of his torso. Arousal waved between them, their hands exploring one another in an unapologetic aggressiveness.

She slipped her thigh between his legs, his hardon unmistakable under the now taut pants.

He moaned pressing it against her leg and—

"Please, no sex on the elevator," screeched the unseen security guard through the intercom, cutting the laugh short.

Pulling apart, Jack cleared his throat as she straightened her miniskirt.

"Shit," muttered Kendall.

"Does that happen often?" Jack rubbed the back of his neck, staring toward the elevator camera.

"Dammit, Jay! Why you gotta ruin my fun," flustered Kendall as the elevator dinged and the doors opened.

"Love you too, Kendall!" The security guard laughed as the intercom crackled.

Kendall flipped a middle finger at the camera and stormed out. Jack rushed to catch up to her. She couldn't decide if the heat in her face was from her arousal or embarrassment.

How could I forget the fucking camera! This must be the third time now that they've caught me making out, hot and heavy.

"You know the security guards?" Jack walked parallel with her, following her through the columns of yellow lights.

"They make themselves known." She laughed. "And it doesn't help that I've him down at least twice in the last year or so. Something about a man in uniform driving a golf cart reminds me of a mall cop doesn't exactly do it for me."

"I see." Jack nodded, hmphing to himself. "So, where's your car?"

"Over here next to..." The lights of her Jetta blinked as Kendall hit her unlock button. "...Gaston. Dammit. I should have known." *I must've been in such a rush, I didn't see that creeper watching me from his car.* "I got an idea, if you're into it."

"Well, I'm really into you at this very moment," retorted Jack.

"Fuck me on his car," she blurted, tugging him by his shirt, pulling it free from his pants.

"Wait..." Jack looked at her car, then at the one she was scooting atop the hood. "The Mercedes? You want me to fuck you atop... Gaston's Mercedes?"

"That's right, my Jolly Green Giant." Her feet left the ground as she pulled him against the car. "Fuck me on his car, right here, right now."

"We just met..." Jack's voice broke into a panic. "What about the car alarm?"

"I bet his alarm settings are set so low you can pound me until we make this bitch rock." She slipped her miniskirt up her thighs until her pink, lacey underwear caught his gaze. "Besides, I came to the party hoping for a quick hook up... and after that rescue, I want to show you my gratitude."

Judging by his facial expression, he's never done something like this before, even though he secretly wants to. This is your chance, Jack! Show me some grit!

Jack covered his mouth, his face visibly thinking as he peered across the parking lot. His cock still strained against his pants, and Kendall wanted to see exactly how much of that bulge was length versus girth. She unfastened the first button of her blouse, then the next, bringing his attention back to her. A matching pink-lace bra poised her amble breast, while her dark nipples peeked between the lacey gaps.

As her shirt laid open, a sound escaped him as if his favorite meal had been set before him.

"I'd like to see you after tonight," he confessed.

"Then when we're done here, give me your number..." She reached for her bra's front latch. *This damn bra's uncomfortable as hell, but the easy access in the heat of the moment is well worth it!*

Her plump breasts lay exposed in the cool air, erecting her nipples. Jack closed the gap, groping the pillow of soft flesh, carefully pinching each nipple. His lips pressed hard against hers. She could feel his hard cock underneath the fabric as he grinded against her pussy. Having his body between her knees made her ache as his hands fell away.

The heat of hands slid up her thighs as she deepened the kiss.

His cock jumped where it pressed into her.
I want you so bad. Give me more...

She lashed out, coaxing his tongue to explore her mouth only to suckle it instead. Arousal waved through them; her breasts pressed hard against his chest as their hearts raced one another. His fingers rubbed against her opening, her panties leaving nothing to the imagination. He rubbed hard and aggressive until she moaned into his mouth. Once more, she pulled him against her, relishing the fire building between them.

Her lacy panties soaked in the rising excitement, her pussy throbbing with want.

Jack broke the kiss as his fingers shoved her panties aside, slipping two fingers inside. She shivered with pleasure, exhilarated by the heat of his breath against her neck. The soft warmth of his lips added to the slow thrusting of his fingers. He burnt his way across her collarbone, travelling in rhythm to his stroking. Kendall's skin pimpled, her imagination painting scenes of how those same lips would feel on her more sensitive places.

"Are you sure about this?" he whispered into her ear in a silky voice, and she inhaled swift. "I've got a condom if you're serious about this."

"Yes..." She moaned as his fingers stroked in and out, gaining speed. "Quick... before Gaston arrives..." She bit her lips, muffling a shriek of ecstasy as he rubbed her in all the right places. "Before I come..."

At last, Jack pulled away, unfastening his pants. She could... *Holy beanstalk!*

She blinked her eyes several times. *Is his long, girthy cock real or some part of my phantom erotic dream.*

He unfurled a Pasante Super King-sized condom over the tallest erection she had ever seen in person. Pulling her from the car, he flipped her around. She yelped as her breast pressed into the Mercedes' cool, metal hood. Fingers tugged her underwear down and rubbed her already dripping, wet pussy. She was on her tippy toes as he pressed the tip of his monstrous cock against her, then slowly sliding it inside, gauging how far he could go.

"Oh..." breathed Kendall, his cock filling her.

She hummed with each pull as it retreated, then slowly reentered, each one gaining more depth than the last. Her legs shook, bringing her chills of pleasure with each rotation. Panting against the hood, she watched his reflection, his intense focus on its waxed surface as he watched himself slide in and out, making her tighten. His head tilted, fighting the overwhelming pleasure rushing through him.

Jack's fingers gripped her hips, his cock throbbing deep inside her. "I'll start slow, but we have to be fast before someone sees us."

This time, he completely slid his length out before pushing back in.

Kendall moaned, her pussy squeezing around him. "Don't be slow. You feel fucking amazing."

He laughed. "As tight as you keep squeezing me, I won't last much longer, baby."

"You said make it quick." She pushed herself into an arch like a cat stretching in the sun, forcing his cock to slide in deeper as she pressed her ass against his waist. "Fuck me, Jack."

He arched an eyebrow. "No one's ever climbed my beanstalk so eagerly before."

"Stop. You're ruining the moment with that cheesy line." She laughed. "Just give me what we both want, big daddy."

"As you wish..."

The heavy panting soon turned into moaning and humming as he continued to push in and out, hard and fast. His huge cock filled her and rubbed into places she never knew existed. The spot she often reached with only her toys were being rubbed by his huge dick. She could feel the rig of his cap and... *I will peak hard at this...* She bit her lip, eye clenched shut as she came. *Yes! YES!* His cock was hard as a rock now, and in a few more strokes, he pushed hard into her with his own moan.

Breathless, they froze, still throbbing from their peaking orgasms. Then a ding from the elevator echoed through parking garage, ending their ecstasy.

"SHIT." Jack pulled out of her, making her gasp before tossing the condom onto the ground between the cars. "Well, uh, I guess..."

"Thank you, Jack," Gaston's voice echoed through the garage, sending Kendall to shove pass Jack and slide into the driver side of her car. "I'll get your number from Pearl!"

"W-wait." Jack rushed to zip up his pants, marveling over the breast-prints reflecting off the Mercedes' black hood. "My number... She doesn't..."

Kendall was backing out of the parking spot when he saw Gaston in the distance, making out with a girl at the elevators. "Well, shit. Guess I better go before he notices me."

Kendall glanced at the awkward wave in her rearview. *SHIT! I should have gotten his number before.* She wiggled in her seat. *Oh, God, I am still riding out the orgasm that man gave me, and I want more. Pearl, you better have his number!*

It's Getting Hot in Here

> *"What have you done with my golden hen?"*

The air conditioning had completely stopped... *again.*

She glared toward the overhead vent in her tiny office with disdain. Kendall had fought the owners over budget cuts and forcing the damned, outdated piece of equipment to last for another year. Frowning to herself, she thought, *it wouldn't be so bad if my office wasn't connected to a fucking greenhouse!*

Standing up, she stretched and shuddered as a droplet of sweat snaked down her spine. Unbuttoning her work polo, she sighed, wishing there were more than three measly slots at the top. She marched out of her office and into the greenhouse's stifling, humid heat. Travelling down the length of the main lane was the only way to reach the owner's office where a brand-new air conditioner had been installed two years prior. Stopping at the door, she inhaled deep, securing her commanding aura in place. Cracking her neck, she at last banged on the door like someone from a SWAT team before a raid.

It swung open and her father grinned. "Why, Kendall, what brings you to this side of the greenhouse?"

"Well, Da..." She cleared her throat. *Keep it business. This isn't Dad, this is one of the owners.* "Mr. Warden," she corrected. "The air conditioner is done for."

Despite his reflective reading glasses obscuring his eyes, she knew he'd dodge the issue. *Again.* "I see... I'll tell you what..."

Kendall crossed her arms, waiting for the distraction or excuse he'd cook up this time.

"I'll get with Bo Smith and see what he can do about this."

She snorted. "I'd rather see an air conditioner man hunched over that outside unit, handing you an estimate to replace that archaic thing. It's been here longer than I've walked this earth, and I'm not exaggerating."

He nodded, spinning them around to walk the humid greenhouse again. "I understand," he assured her. "In that case, could you give the new guy the grand tour and make sure he completes all that HR stuff? He starts today."

And there's the distraction. Granted, he'd rather deal with a new air conditioner than train anyone for anything around here. Kendall narrowed her eyes, her voice flat and agitated at best. "And who did you hire to do *what* exactly?"

"J... J... Jay Spudnik?" He winced. "It's a J-name. Anyhow, he'll help us rework the heating and cooling computer systems. Some sort of software engineer that isn't afraid to get his hands dirty. Real nice guy, tall as hell. This way, we figured you and the rest of the staff wouldn't have to rush out here in the middle of the night during a cold snap anymore. Dealing with the heaters or closing and opening the vents in the middle of the night is a pain. I'm too old for that."

And why do I question his intent on this? Goosebumps rolled across her skin. *And my gut is screaming. Something's off about this...*

"I thought you said you were hot?" Her father chuckled, and she rolled her eyes. "Just kidding, Kendall. I'm serious. Old Frances across the building had already railed me on the failing AC system. Bo and I will get you, office girls, squared away. Promise. Just, do me this favor and train the new guy by starting him on those HR videos."

"Fine." At last, she unfolded her arms. "When does he arrive?"

"Now. He's already waiting in Frances' office." He stopped midway through the greenhouse, waving her on.

Rolling her eyes once more, she muttered remarks about her father's levels of procrastination he had mastered. She opened Frances' office and closed her eyes. The blast of heat radiating from the open door was stifling. *The greenhouse feels cooler!*

"Fran, would you like me to prop open the door?" she called out, searching the ground for the door stopper.

"At first I didn't want to." The elderly woman's voice sounded exasperated. "But I can't work like this. Especially if the open door gets my papers soggy. But that blast of cool air says I'll cook in this oven of an office if I don't."

"I can give you a dehumidifier to lower the humidity level, but it's hotter than the greenhouse in here, honey." She spotted the doorstop between the wall and filing cabinet.

"Dammit I'll have to get on all fours to reach that." Dropping down, she stretched her fingertips, barely grazing her target.

"I can move it." Jack's voice sent her heart racing. *Oh no, the hot beanstalk man from a few months ago. It can't be.* Her fingers clawed it closer, and she gripped it.

"I g-got it." She stood, keeping her back faced him. *SHIT! This can't be happening!*

He cleared his throat, admitting in a low, confident voice, "Wasn't that the same position you were in the last time I saw you? Pearl wouldn't give me your number, but this almost seems like... fate."

Her heated face surged with a rising tide of anger and embarrassment. "She should have." Spinning with renewed confidence, she slapped the doorstop in his hand. "Prop open the door while I grab the dehumidifier, Jack."

"Ah, so you do remember my name after all, Kendall." The goofy grin and the glint in his eyes said he intended to pick up exactly where they'd left off.

"And to be fair, she said she couldn't find your number," she confessed.

"That's because she doesn't have my number," he called after her.

Kendall's heart pounded hard. *This will be interesting.* Pulling a humidifier from the janitor's closet, she shoved it into Frances' office. Her mind racing, memories of their rushed, steamy session atop Gaston's Mercedes boiled to the surface. She hadn't been satisfied; she had wanted more... *dammit, I even went home and...*

He grabbed the humidifier and lugged it into his arms with a wink. The bulge of his biceps in his short sleeve sent her body ablaze with want.

What the hell am I going to do? Do I pick up where we left off? Not the fucking part, but do I want a relationship with him? I barely know him... Come on, girl. Let's be real. You let this man bend you over a Mercedes. At this point, all formalities are out the window, aren't they?

She waited at the door, listening to how he politely addressed the old woman, and without any direction, had her setup in no time. Jack returned to the doorway, flashing a handsome smile that could make any girl swoon at how tall and thick he'd looked. *I wonder what he looks completely undressed...*

Shit. My mind's will be stuck in the gutter all damn day.

"I didn't realize you were in the plant business," he started, rubbing the back of his neck as she stared up at him.

Oh, how I imagined those lips on my...

"Breasts. I mean, Bromeliads," she clarified. "We travel all over the world for shows and conventions in fact."

He smirked, trying to remain professional as he replied, "Yeah, Mr. Warden had said you have greenhouses all over the place, including Costa Rica, right?" His flirtatious tone had fully faded now. He was talking business this time.

Thank you! BUSINESS. THINK BUSINESS, ME!

"There, and partners in Holland." She motioned for him to follow. "You already met Fran, the accounts manager. Janey, the scheduler and secretary, is on vacation and their assistant is Sammy. She's either at lunch or on PTO. The four of us work on this side of the greenhouse. The owners, Mr. Warden and Mr. Smith, have offices on the other end. As for the bathrooms, there are two here, but we keep the left one locked. Over here is my office. I'm the Sales Manager and further down, are the other sales representatives. Halfway down is the breakroom, the Greenhouse Manger's office, and the server room..." He followed her in silence, looking at everything she pointed to with a stern expression. "...that'll be your office. Though I have no idea what state it's in after they fired Greg."

"Fired?" Jack asked, curiosity riding on his voice. "What did he do?"

"Lied to the owners. Said he was actively reprogramming the fan vents parameters, only to discover he had no power flowing into his office for an entire *three* days."

"Wow." He hissed, gritting his teeth before prying further. "And how did you figure that out?"

Kendall smirked, shrugging. "Maybe someone flipped the breaker, wondering how long it would take for the lazy ass to figure it out. I suspect he was watching YouTube on his cell or sleeping the hours away."

"But how was he clocking in and out?" Jack followed her into her office, the heat of the room startling. "Holy smokes."

"Yeah, hold on." Walking toward the window, she lifted the blinds to reveal a window unit and plugged it in, turning it on. "It will take some time for it to catch up. I should've turned it on before I marched down there..."

"Why don't you keep it plugged in?" Sweat beaded on his forehead as he whistled, fanning himself.

She pointed at the overhead vent and drawled, "Because *this* is supposed to cool the room."

"Oh," he said, reaching up. "It's actually blowing hot air. Want me to close it?"

"Yeah, then come sit." She motioned to her chair and desk. "I'll get you started on the mandatory human resource videos. Then we'll see what state your office is in. Be warned, it may be just as hot. Let's pray the AC man gets here today and replaces that ancient unit."

She leaned over him, both of them hot and sweaty as she clicked on the computer. In the screen's reflection, she saw his eyes lock with her cleavage hovering over his shoulder. A grin curled her lips. *Yeah, it seems we both were unhappy with how that night ended. Fate, you say? Maybe...* She reached down and grabbed his hand, placing it on the mouse. Flashes of how he gripped her breasts and hips made her pussy throb.

They locked eyes.

Jack's body stiffened as he froze. She could tell he was feeling the same reaction. Kendall's body moved before she knew what she'd done.

Her lips pressed hard against his. Strong arms wrapped around her as he deepened the kiss. Their tongues licked at one another until he suckled on hers, making promises as to what else he would suck if given a chance. Her body buzzed with arousal. The chair squeaked as she leaned harder into him, shattering her desire.

She flew back a few long strides, covering her mouth. "I'm sorry, I don't know what came over me..." She lowered her eyes toward the ground, afraid to see the expression on his face. *SHIT.*

Jack laughed, and at last, offered, "Will you at least take my number this time?"

"Y-yes." She grabbed her cell phone and keys from the desk. "Give it to me now. Jack... Spriggins, right?"

He sighed, grinning from ear to ear. "Yeah, 321-555-1234. That's my cell phone. Maybe after work we could... have dinner or grab a drink?"

"Y-yes. If you—"

"We will be covering Sexual Harrass—" The video had finally loaded and started to play.

"Wow," he marveled, rolling closer to pause it. "Is the internet really that slow here?"

"Yeah, but I suspect he didn't run the wires right." She shrugged, making her way toward the door. *I can't be in the same room or this man or I might find myself bending over my desk this time!* "Um, I need to take care of some things. This should keep you busy for at least a good hour or so."

"Usually how this goes." By the smirk on his face, she knew he found her nervous body language adorable. "I'll text you if I need you, then?"

"Y-yeah." She spun on her heels. "Just text me."

She was out the door, breathing easier as it shut behind her. Eyeing the locked bathroom, she glanced down at her keys. *So glad I thought to grab these.* Looking around, no one seemed to be working this afternoon. *Shit, that's right. It's New Year's Eve. Most of them already asked for PTO or already heading home at any moment.*

41

Dammit, dad! This is why you ditched the new employee training on me! SO YOU COULD LEAVE EARLY!

Gripping the keys tight, she marched toward the locked bathroom and slipped inside. She stared at herself in the mirror, flipping on the fluorescent lights. Heated desire filled her thoughts, making her body ache. *I can't walk out of here until I've blown off this steam.* Opening a drawer, there sat a purple vibrator, still hooked to the charger. Her greatest secret revealed. When in need of releasing her work stress and frustration, she'd slip inside the recently renovated bathroom and pleasure herself.

No one ever questioned why she kept it under lock and key. *One of the few perks of being the owner's daughter.*

"Well, little buddy... with Jack working here, you might be seeing a lot more action than what either of us signed up for." She reached into the shirt pocket, searching for her golden pen but found it empty. "Huh, must have left that on my desk."

4

Avoiding the Giant

"There you are again with your fee-fi-fo-fum."

K endall double-checked the locks and froze. Outside, she could hear Jack's voice and... *crap! It's dad!*

"Where's Kendall?" Mr. Warden chuckled to himself. "Well, I guess the air—"

Kendall dropped the vibrator into the drawer and slammed it shut before rushing out of the bathroom. Jack and Mr. Warden jumped, wide-eyed.

She narrowed her eyes at her father, crossing her arms with murderous intent. "What about the air conditioner?" Kendall gave a deep growl.

"I was going to say," started Mr. Warden, dodging her gaze. "They'll be here tomorrow." He turned his attention to Jack and said, "How's your training coming along?"

Jack rubbed his neck, shooting a confused glance at Kendall. "Well, I'm almost done with all the HR formalities. Kendall already gave me the grand tour, and I look forward to seeing what I can do about this shotty internet connection. I've had to refresh a few times, so it's a tad bit agonizing, to be honest."

Mr. Warden's eyes widened, his voice filled with excitement as he said, "You can fix the internet?"

"Maybe." Jack laughed. "Judging by the looks of the IT room, it will need a wire or two replaced."

"Please. I'd like to make an order for my clients without having to double checking whether it disconnect midway or not." Kendall unfolded her arms, her abrasive demeanor fading. "I figured you'd leave with the rest of the staff."

"Well, I came to say bye," confessed Mr. Warden. "And your mother wanted to know if you were still coming over to watch fireworks by the lake?"

Shit! I wanted to go out with...

"Ah, father and daughter," Jack interjected. "I was trying to figure out if you two were related and how but I was too shy to ask and come off as rude."

Mr. Warden chuckled, throwing an arm over Kendall's shoulders. "We do our best to remain professional here at Firebird Nurseries. So proud of my baby girl. She used to be a greenhouse laborer and worked her way up to Sales Manager."

"Proud indeed." Jack smirked at her as she brushed her dad's arms off. "Well, go home, old man, and let me finish training Jack."

"Fine, fine..." Mr. Warden waved her off.

They watched him leave, an awkward silence filling the air.

Jack and her briefly exchanged glares before he said at last, "I guess I should finish that video. But before that... I'll take a look at the wires real fast in IT room, is that ok?"

"Uh, sure. If you think you can fix it, that would be great." The buzz of arousal blossomed through her again, her thoughts reverting back to the drawer and the purple prize awaiting her. "I'm going to... uh..." She pointed and reached for the door. "Just heard Dad and know how slimy he can be... back to what I was about to do... I guess..."

"R-right." Pivoting, he marched down the hall, while she escaped into the bathroom once more.

Crap! He's gotta be feeling just as aroused as I am. That look in his eyes... I'm melting in my panties! She settled into position atop the pristine closed toilet, pants and panties abandoned on the floor. Dripping lube on

46

the purple vibrator, she held the button and it buzzed in her hand.

Spreading her legs, she let her mind slip back to the Mercedes, the kiss in the office, and... *If only he'd fuck me in my office, but the walls are too thin for the pounding I want.*

First, she slid the vibrating tip over her clit, back and forth across her opening, the sensation enlightening. The tension in her shoulders started to fade as she began to relax and enjoy the release she aimed for. After a few teasing glides, the vibrator ran slick with lube and her own rising wetness as the tip rubbed against her swelling clit from her building orgasm. Her sensitive nipples became erect, pressing through her bra and shirt, adding to the desires racing through her mind.

Oh, how I wanted to feel him lick my pussy...

Her breathing quickened, her heart racing. She slid the purple appendage downward, pressing and threatening to enter her slick folds. *Oh, how girthy he felt knocking at the door, so slow and...* Shifting her position, she wanted

47

to open further in anticipation for penetrating herself over and—

Bling!

She ignored her phone, the text notification ringing out. Closing her eyes again—

Bling! Bling!

Clenching her eyes shut, she pushed the vibrator inside, slow as the buzzing made her pussy tighten against the soft—

Bling! Bli-Bling!

Closing her thighs, cheeks puffed out, she shuffled in her pant pockets for her phone. "I swear, this better be an emergency..."

[Jack: You coming out of the bathroom any time this week?]

Kendall's face heated. *Dammit, I'm taking my time, but I thought he'd be stuck with slow internet...*

[Kendall: I thought you were playing with wires? Don't you have a video to finish?]

[Jack: Internet is out. There's a rat nest in the box. Like *literally* a rat and his collection of

48

candy bar wrappers in there, but I don't know what to do.]

[Kendall: Ask Fran.] She settled back into place.

[Jack: She's gone.]

[Kendall: Yeah, they have a half day today. I imagine it's just us now.]

She settled back into place, the vibrator still buzzing where she held it between her legs, making her body heat as it excited her pussy.

[Jack: I can't stop thinking about you.]

Licking her lips, she opened her thighs and returned to teasing her clit. She slid her thumb over the touchscreen. *I wonder what the chances are that he'd be willing to entertain the idea of this...*

[Kendall: I can't lie. I've been thinking about that night...]

[Jack: Oh yeah? I wasn't done but you left in a hurry. Shame you don't have a lock on your office door. We should fix that.]

[Kendall: That's why the bathroom has one and I've got the only key.]

There was a long pause. Pushing the button to increase the vibrations, she circled her clit more aggressively, stronger until she could feel herself creep closer to an orgasm.

[Jack: Tell me what you're doing. Right now. I'm agonizing not being able to kiss you again.]

[Kendall: Playing with myself while I think of you.]

Another long pause and she grinned. He was being cautious, and it only made her bite her lip in anticipation. *What will you with that knowledge, hmm? Mr. Jack? Will you play with me? Are you jealous I can touch myself and you can't?*

[Jack: I would trail kisses down that gorgeous body and suck on your nipples until you beg me to stop.]

[Kendall: Show me that monster beanstalk again, Jack. I want to climb your one-eyed giant again.]

[Jack: *Dick pic.*]

She inhaled, slowly sliding the vibrator into her pussy. The image was fresh, the terrazzo flooring and her desk in the background. He was hard just thinking about her touching herself. Just like her, he was thinking about fucking her all over again. She thrusted the vibrator in and out, eyes on the hardened cock she had dreamed about having inside her once more.

[Jack: I want to see how wet you get as you think of me.]

Swallowing, she pulled the vibrator out, shutting it off and placing it atop the vanity. Adjusting once more, her fingers spread her folds and after a few attempts, she managed to take a selfie, revealing the state of her swollen, dripping clit.

[Kendall: *Pussy pic.* I can't stop touching myself. I want you.]

His paused reply made her grin. Her finger circled her pink jewel, her legs shaking with the rise of her incoming orgasm. She scrolled back to his cock, a rush of arousal waving through

51

her. In a flash, she was bent over the hood of Gaston's Mercedes once more. Jack's rock-hard dick sliding inside her, jumping and throbbing in response to her own pussy tightening.

[Jack: Send more pics. Show me those lips, those breasts, those fingers dipping in places I want to be in right now.]

She inhaled swift. The words resonated as her pleasure buzzed through her.

[Kendall: *Pic of her biting her lips.* Talk dirty to me.]

[Jack: I want to feel those lips wrapped around my cock, feel that dirty tongue wiggling underneath my dick.]

[Kendall: *A single breast and erect nipple.*]

[Jack: I want to suckle those titties and play with your pussy.]

[Kendall: *Closeup of her fingers dipping into her pussy.*]

[Jack: I want to bend you over and pound you until you beg me to stop.]

[Kendall: You are terrible at this.]

[Jack: Yeah, sexting is not my strong suit.]

Knock-knock-knock!

Kendall straightened, staring at the door in alarm.

[Jack: Fee-fi-fo-fum... may I come in and join?]

She laughed. *Be careful what you wish for.*

[Kendall: As long as the giant promises to gobble me up.]

The door opened and shut fast; the lock flipped with a loud *clack.*

Crap, I forgot to lock it earlier!

"I've been waiting to get you alone after work but..." He smirked at her provocative position, spread-eagle atop the toilet seat as her phone hit the floor. "...it seems you couldn't wait that much longer either."

5

Begging for More

*"Be he alive or be he dead, I'll grind his
bones to make my bread."*

A chill snaked up Kendall's spine. She jerked
up, standing in alarm. In a blink of an
eye, her sexting session shifted into a secret
office rendezvous. *This is a first...* The way her
heart raced, pounding loud and fierce, her
chest aching.

Jack flicked his eyebrows high, his grin ever
growing on his face. Tugging at the buttons on
his shirt, she followed his fingers as they filleted
his shirt open, revealing the muscles she had

felt months before. Kendall couldn't contain her smirk as they raced downward where his pants were already unbuckled, tightening around his hardening cock.

She scoffed. "It seems someone else couldn't wait either," she said as he unzipped, and his dick stood erect, free from his pants.

"Come here." His voice was deep and soft all at once, commanding her as she dared to close the gap.

If this goes as wild as last time... The heat of his torso underneath her hands added to the fiery passion she could no longer deny. *I've never felt chemistry this hot and hungry for anyone before.*

Jack cupped her jaw and pressed his lips firmly against hers. The kiss was slow, teasing, and loving. His lips parted, and she dipped her tongue between as a sacrifice to give her more. Hot hands moved to hold her hostage against him. His hard cock throbbed between them. *He wants me now, but he's taking it slow, unlike last time. Yes, show me this other side... give me the time I denied you...*

"Show me what I missed out that night," she dared him, her voice sultry as he began to kiss her neck.

Jack stayed silent as he worshipped her body with his lips. Removing her polo shirt, he shed his own as she abandoned her bra at last. His hands gripped her hips, guiding her between him and the vanity before sitting her on top. A halo of lights crowned her head as she leaned back to take him all in as his pants fell to the floor. The icy mirror against her back wasn't the reason for her shivers and moans. His hungry, hazel eyes told her where he wanted to go next. So she parted her thighs, giving him full access to everything her body wanted to offer him.

Closing her eyes, she wanted to savor every touch. Hands glided up her thighs, teasingly close as they slid up her torso and cupped her breast. The heat of his breath against her pussy made her tense with anticipation. With a twist of her nipples, the hands retreated the way they had traveled. Squeezing her thighs, he pushed them wider. His silken tongue ran across her opening, hot and wet. She inhaled swift, the sensation exhilarating. He moaned as he licked slow and intentional, the tip of his tongue circling her clit once or twice before repeating the pattern that made her legs twitch.

Kendall arched her back and reached down. She held him into her, returning his moaning with her own. Her legs jittered with the oncoming orgasm that teetered on the edge as he continued eating. His tongue thrusted deep into her, wiggling as her fingers clawed the back of his head. *So hot, so soft... I'm so wet, and he just laps me up with such greed.*

"Don't stop," she breathed, shifting the tilt of her hip to give him a better angle. "So... so close..."

He licked upward, playing and rubbing her swollen jewel as if needing to be taste at every angle. Again, her legs shook. Hands rode over her torso to grope her breasts firm. Kendall's breath caught. Lips wrapped tight around her clit, sucking hard and long, ringing the devil's doorbell.

She abandoned his head, throwing her arm over her mouth to muffle her squeal. *I can't be too loud, just in case…*

A harder suckle, and she raised her knees. Her teeth bit into her arm, back arching. Two fingers slid inside, thrusting, and she peaked instantly for him. He didn't stop. Lips surrounding the swollen pearl of flesh, her pussy tightened on his thrusting fingers, the sound of her wetness filling the room.

Jack's moaning added to her peaking orgasm. Kendall's body tensed, folding forward. With a pop, he released her clit and kissed her. She could taste herself on his tongue as he kept thrusting in and out of her.

Yes! YES! This man has the golden touch!

He rose up before her, his erection hard and veiny. His fingers left her, but the tip of his cock pressed against her throbbing pussy. She wrapped her legs around him, pulling him into her as they touched foreheads, pushing him inside her pulsing pussy. His body waved, grinding into her, the muscles in his torso tensing and relaxing as he banged her slow and rhythmic. *Oh, how I wanted another ride on this monster cock!*

They stared into each others' eyes, seeing each other's pleasure.

"Shit, condom," Kendall panicked, lost in the heat of the moment.

"I already took care of it while I was enjoying my appetizer." His arms wrapped around her, pulling her further away from the vanity ledge.

The counter began to wobble, threatening to break away from the wall. Jack spun them around, carrying Kendall until her back hit the opposite wall. She could see over his shoulder, his bare back and his tight ass in the mirror where she had sat seconds before. The way his muscles waved, tensing and loosening in a way that, was hypnotic to watch in the reflection.

He gripped her knee, raising her leg higher so he could grind deeper into her pussy. She moaned, and he began kissing her neck once more. Her entire body heated, buzzing with another rising orgasm. His cock throbbed, hardening with each thrust as her pussy tightened in response.

At last, Jack panted, "I'm about to come."

She begged, "Please, a little longer."

He pulled out, shrinking before her as he brought her leg over his shoulder. His arm glided across her torso, groping her breast. Once more the silken heat of his tongue ran across her pussy. Her breath caught. Finger dove between her swollen folds as his lips wrapped around her pink pearl. *So sensitive!* It was driving her wild as she clawed at his shoulders. Kendall couldn't decide if she wanted to fight him off or allow him more access. *He's driving me wild!*

Again, the tip of his tongue ran across her opening, from where his fingers stroked against her swollen clit.

"Don't stop," she breathed. "So close..."

Another orgasm began to build. She pushed against his hand, grinding to deepen his fingering. Her pussy tightens around them.

His other fingers tightly pinch her nipple. Picking up pace, Jack suckles hard and long on her clit. Her clawing hands rack across his back and shoulders, abandoning their fight to keep him away and encouraging him to continue.

Covering her mouth, she screams into her palm. Her knees shake with her orgasm as it comes, hard and fast.

Flawlessly, Jack abandons his play and pushes his hard cock back inside her. She arches her back, no longer worried about containing her scream as he moans. He quickens his pounding, in and out, in and out, so hard and fast. Jack's arms wrapped around her, pulling her into him as he begins to suckle her breast.

Her entire body vibrates with pleasure unlike anything she's ever experienced before.

"Yes! Oh fuck yes!" she cried out.

"You're so tight when you come..." he panted between each thrust. "Fucking come for me one more time... I'm so close."

"Don't stop, don't stop..." she breathed, clawing him into her.

Lips hot around her nipple, he teases her with his teeth, and she screamed, visceral and wild. Her orgasm peaks further than its predecessors. He gripped her leg hard, his moaning loud as he pressed himself deeper into her, their bodies tense and tight against each other. Their shared throbbing made their pleasurable higher and linger.

Minutes pass, both frozen and afraid to move in their sensitive state.

At last, his gaze meets hers and he grins wide. "You still want to have dinner?" he teased.

"How about you join me at my parents? Fireworks and free food," she offered.

"Only if we're going steady," he countered.

Laughing, she covered her face. "Yes, Jack. I suppose I can't say no after fucking you twice."

"Good, I guess I can return your golden pen."

Kendall made a bewildered face. "Why did you take my pen?"

"Well, I needed an excuse to come see you again and took it while we were kissing." He laughs, explaining, "Don't you know the story, *Jack and the Beanstalk*? He was a thief after all..."

THE END

Honey Cummings

A passionate, award-winning author of Fantasy, Honey has turned her aim towards erotica. Blending everyday scenarios and crafting them into steamy, blood-boiling moments for every shade of audience. Whether you want something short and hot like a student-teacher hook up to the more paranormal flair where Sleep with Sasquatch has unexpected bonus, look forward to erotic short stories, novellas, and hopefully a Trilogy in the future. Honey's debut erotic short landed No. 3 in Urban Erotica and continues to satisfy readers time and time again. Be sure to leave her a review and let her know what you think!

https://www.amazon.com/Honey-Cummings/e/
B07WFX5FDX

www.AuthorHoneyCummings.com

instagram.com/authorhoneycummings

twitter.com/HoneyCummings2

facebook.com/
Author-Honey-Cummings-101408818012749

MORE HONEY CUMMINGS BOOKS

Sleeping with Sasquatch
Cuddling with Chupacabra
Naked with New Jersey Devil

Laying with the Lady in Blue
Wanton Woman in White
Beating it with Bloody Mary

Beau and Professor Bestialora
The Goat's Gruff
Goldie and Her Three Beards
Pied Piper's Pipe
Princess Pea's Bed
Pinocchio and the Blow Up Doll
Jack's Beanstalk

Curses & Crushes

Unwrap Me: An XXX-mas Anthology

CHASTITY VELDT

Molly in Milwaukee
Irene in Idianapolis
Lydia in Louisville
Natasha in Nashville
Alyssa in Atlanta

GAY EROTICA

GRAYSON ACE
How I Got Here
First Year Out of the Closet
You're Only a Top?
You're Only a Bottom?
I Think I'm a Serial Swiper
Lookin' in All the Wrong Places

LEO SPARX
Before Alexander
Claiming Alexander
Taming Alexander
Saving Alexander

4HorsemenPublications.com

www.ingramcontent.com/pod-product-compliance
Lightning Source LLC
Chambersburg PA
CBHW020722130726
47899CB00011B/1022